DISCARDED
from the Nashville Public Library

KENNETH GRAHAME'S

The RELUCTANT DRAGON

RETOLD BY ROBERT D. SAN SOUCI

ILLUSTRATED BY JOHN SEGAL

ORCHARD BOOKS • AN IMPRINT OF SCHOLASTIC INC. • NEW YORK

HALTON HILLS PUBLIC LIBRARIES

Text copyright © 2004 by Robert D. San Souci ♦ Illustrations copyright © 2004 by John Segal ♦ All rights reserved. Published by Orchard Books, an imprint of Scholastic Inc. ORCHARD BOOKS and design are registered trademarks of Watts Publishing Group, Ltd., used under license. SCHOLASTIC and associated logos are trademarks and/or registered trademarks of Scholastic Inc. No part of this publication may be reproduced, or stored in a retrieval system, or transmitted in any form or by any means, electronic, mechanical, photocopying, recording, or otherwise, without written permission of the publisher. For information regarding permission, write to Orchard Books, Scholastic Inc., Permissions Department, 557 Broadway, New York, NY 10012.

LIBRARY OF CONGRESS CATALOGING-IN-PUBLICATION DATA AVAILABLE

ISBN: 0-439-45581-2

10 9 8 7 6 5 4 3 2 1   04 05 06 07 08

Printed in Singapore   46 ♦ Reinforced binding for library use First Scholastic edition, April 2004 ♦ Illustrations for the book were done using an 8h lead drawing pencil, and Schmincke watercolors on Arches 90-lb. cold press watercolor paper.. The display type was hand-lettered by John Segal. The text was set in 15-pt. Bernhard Modern.

Book design by SKC

– for ELLEN MAGER –
BOOKSELLER par EXCELLENCE,
TIRELESS ADVOCATE OF LITERACY,
and, BEST OF all, MY FRIEND.

– R.S.S.

~~~~~

FOR Emily and JOSHUA,
MY TWO FAVORITE READERS.

– JS

Rolling, Grass–
Covered Hills

The Shepherd

The Boy

Long ago, in England, a shepherd, his wife, and their son lived in

a cottage between a pretty little village and rolling, grass-covered hills.

The shepherd spent much of his time in the high meadows, with the

sun, stars, and his sheep for company. His son, when not helping his

father or mother, spent most of his time reading natural history and

fairy tale books that he borrowed from neighboring gentlemen and

clergy. His parents were proud of his learning, and they treated him as

an equal. They knew that book learning could come in handy — as the

boy had shown on many occasions.

One evening, the shepherd greeted his family and exclaimed, "We're ruined! I can't take our sheep to graze in the hills any more!"

"Catch your breath," Jack said sensibly, putting down the book he was reading. "Then tell us what's wrong."

"We're RUINED!"

"You know that cave at the meadow's end? The one the sheep stay clear of?" said the shepherd breathlessly. "Well, for days it's been giving off noises — sighs and grunts and snores — from deep inside. Now, noises are only noises, but today I saw the cause of them."

"Saw what?" his wife asked, beginning to share her husband's fear.

"IT! Sticking halfway out of the cave as if it were enjoying the cool of the evening. Big as four horses! Covered with blue scales on top and green below! And when he breathed, a flicker of flame danced over his snout. He had his chin on his paws and a grin as though he

"Big as FOUR horses!"

was ever so contented. He had claws, and I'm sure a tail, though I couldn't see the other end of him. But I saw enough to know that I never want to see the like again!"

"Don't worry, Father," said Jack. "It's only a dragon."

"Only a dragon!" cried his father. "What do you know about such things?"

"I know a lot from the books I read," the boy answered quietly. "Just leave this to me. I'll go up tomorrow and talk with him. I've read that some dragons are very reasonable creatures."

So the next day, Jack strolled up to the dragon's cave. He found the creature stretched out in the warm sun, enjoying the view of village and farms and orchards and fields. As he drew near, the boy could hear the beast purring. "Well!" he said to himself in surprise, "none of my books told me that dragons purr!"

"Hello, dragon," Jack called politely.

Seeing it was a boy, the dragon warned, "Don't you throw stones or squirt water or anything."

"I'm not going to hit you," said Jack. "I just wanted to ask how you are. But if you don't want me to stay, I have other things to do."

Jack strolled
up to the
Dragon's cave.

He found the creature stretched
out in the warm sun...

"I'M NOT going to HIT you"

"Don't go off in a huff," the dragon said hastily. "There are plenty of things to occupy me, but it does get a bit dull at times."

"Are you planning to stay long?" asked Jack, sitting on the grass.

"Can't say," said the dragon. "One must think carefully before settling down."

"Then how did you wind up here?" Jack asked.

"I'm not sure. I was bedded down for the night in my own cave, somewhere else. Then there was a shake and a roar and the ground just rolled me along through miles of tunnels until I ended up at the back of this cave, with tumbled rock behind me, and the sun shining into the front. I like the scenery and the people — well, you're the only one I've properly met. So, I'm thinking probably I will settle here."

"What do you do when you're not thinking or looking at the view?"

The dragon suddenly grew bashful. "I compose poems."

"So do I!" cried the boy. "I'm not sure that my mother and father understand my poems, but they always say they're good."

"Are you planning
to stay LONG?"

"There was a
Shake and a Roar..."

"I compose
poems."

"I knew at once that you were an intelligent lad!" said the dragon. "May I recite my newest poem for you?"

"Not right now," said Jack, standing up. "I have chores to do at home. But I'll come back soon and listen."

" you're a dragon, an enemy of the human race. "

"Bring your parents, too. And your neighbors."

"My parents will come," said the boy. "But I'm not at all sure how the neighbors will take to you. The fact is, you're a dragon, an enemy of the human race."

"Nonsense!" said the dragon cheerfully. "I'm too lazy to make enemies."

"Oh, dear!" Jack said worriedly. "Try to understand: I'm afraid that when other people find out about you, they'll come after you with swords and spears. They'll say you're a horrible monster who will lay waste to the countryside."

"They'll come after you..."

"Never!" said the dragon. "Now, can't you listen to just one little poem?"

"I really must go," said the boy. He added sternly, "And do try to realize that most folks will think you are a deadly danger, or you'll find yourself in an awful mess." Then he went off with a wave of his hand.

In the days that followed, Jack introduced his mother and father to his new friend. They often gathered together and listened to the dragon and Jack recite their poems. Sometimes Jack's father and the dragon would play cards while Jack's mother puttered about, tidying the dragon's cave. On occasion, the dragon would lead them all in a sing-along.

They all agreed that it was best to keep things to themselves, since their neighbors were excitable and might try to drive the dragon away with weapons and torches — this being the

play cards

TIDYING

SING-along

WEAPONS and
TORCHES

There was a
dragon nearby ...

WORD SPREAD

usual treatment of monsters who took residence in the area.

But you can't keep a creature as big as four horses and covered in blue and green scales a secret for long. Word spread that there was a dragon nearby and that something must be done about the threat — though no one and nothing had been harmed since his arrival.

Still the townsfolk cried, "The dreadful beast must be destroyed!" But no one was willing to take up sword or spear and face the monster, so the dragon was left to polish his poems and tell Jack stories of olden times.

One day, Jack, running an errand in the village, found the streets crowded with excited people.

"What's up?" Jack asked a friend of his.

"Saint George has heard about our dragon and has come to slay the deadly beast."

Before Jack could respond, a roar rose from the crowd. Down the street rode the knight himself, who had been declared a saint for slaying dragons and saving princesses. He wore gold armor and a plumed helmet, and he carried a golden sword and spear. His face was gentle, yet fierce enough to sink Jack's heart. The boy began running toward the hills.

He found the dragon polishing his scales with a cloth that Jack's mother had given him. "Saint George is coming to battle you!" shouted Jack. "Of course, a big fellow like you can lick him. But he's got a wicked-looking spear, so you'd better be prepared for a terrible fight!"

"What's up?"

"saint George has heard about our DRagoN..."

"... he's GOT a wicked-LookiNg speaR"

"You have to fight him!"

"Bother!" the dragon said, wrinkling his snout. "I won't see him, and that's flat. I'm sure he's not nice. You must tell him to go away at once."

"You have to fight him! He's Saint George. You're the dragon. You'll just have to get it over with, and then you can go back to your poetry."

"I never fight," the dragon said. "You just go and explain things. You have a gift for words. I leave everything to you."

Realizing that he couldn't talk sense to his friend, Jack hurried back to the village inn. There the saint was listening to villager after villager tell fanciful tales of the horrors the dragon had brought upon them. Jack pushed through the crowd and asked politely, "May I say something about the dragon, Saint George?"

"Yes, my boy," said the saint, as the adults listened eagerly. "Have you lost a parent, or a dear brother or sister, to the monster? I promise you, I'll make him suffer for the pain he has caused you."

"Oh, no!" said Jack. "He's a good dragon who loves to think deep thoughts and make up poems. My mother and father think the world of him. He's my friend. It's not at all like the stories they've been telling you!" He pointed at the villagers, who began to drift away.

When they were alone, Saint George said, "I had doubts about some of the stories I was hearing. But they were certainly colorful. Anyhow, I'm sure the dragon must have a good quality or two, if you feel such loyalty to him. But isn't it possible that he's misled you? Perhaps he has some poor princess hidden in his gloomy cavern at this very minute."

Jack shook his head. "He's a gentleman. Couldn't you just go away quietly and leave him alone?" the boy added hopefully.

"Quite against the rules," said the saint.

"Would you just come talk to him?" asked Jack. "Maybe we can think of something."

"It's irregular," said Saint George. But seeing the look on Jack's face, he added, "Very well."

"He's my friend."

"This is Saint George," Jack called as they neared the cave. "Saint George, let me introduce you to the dragon."

"So glad to meet you," said the dragon rather nervously. "Lovely weather we're having."

"Lovely weather we're having."

"Dragon!" said Jack. "We've got more important things to talk about."

"Yes," agreed Saint George in his frank, pleasant way, "I think we'd better take our young friend's advice and talk about how to settle this matter. Why don't we just fight according to the rules, and let the best man – or dragon – win?"

"There's nothing to fight about, and so I won't, and that's that," said the dragon.

"There's NOTHING to Fight ABout, and so I WON't..."

"There must be a fight," said Jack. "People expect it. Saint George is bound by rules. Just think of the poems you could compose about sunlight glinting on your blue and green scales and Saint George's gold armor as you meet in deadly combat."

"Is this really necessary?"

"It would make a striking poem," said the dragon, wavering a bit. "But I find the use of 'deadly' and 'combat' a bit off-putting. Is this really necessary?"

"Yes," said the Saint. "I'm obliged to spear you somewhere, but I don't have to hurt you. Surely you've got a spare place somewhere?"

"Well," said the dragon, "these folds under my neck are so much baggage. You could spear me there, and I'd never even know it."

"You could spear me there, and I'd never even know it"

"I shall lead the defeated creature into town."

"Then I shall lead the defeated creature into town," the saint explained to Jack. "Then there will be a great deal of feasting and cheering and speeches and so on. I'll tell them our scaly friend has seen the error of his ways –"

"And then?" the dragon asked eagerly.

"Then people will celebrate what a miracle it is to have such a monster tamed! You'll become the darling of the day," said the saint.

"Then people will celebrate ..."

HALTON HILLS PUBLIC LIBRARIES

BANNERS

Medals

Dishes

"I'll be popular! I'll become the village mascot! My picture will appear on banners and medals and dishes – oh! And yours, too, of course, Saint George," said the dragon with a bow.

Saint George bowed back.

"If people are going to believe this," said Jack to the dragon, "you'll

"ROAR"

"RAMPAGE"

"Breathe Fire"

have to roar and rampage and breathe fire."

"The roaring and rampaging is easy," said the dragon. "I'm a bit out of practice with fiery blasts. But I'll do the best I can."

When they had laid their plans, Jack went home; the dragon, to his cave; and Saint George, to the inn to await the next day's events.

The next morning, the villagers, alerted by Jack's shouts, began streaming into the hills carrying picnic baskets, eager to see the fatal combat between saint and dragon. When cheering signaled the arrival of the saint on his huge warhorse, Jack whispered into the darkness of the cave, "Are you ready?"

"Tut! Tut!" answered the dragon. "I've been practicing my fire-breathing techniques since dawn. See if I don't give my public just what they want!" He began with a mutter mingled with snorts, then raised it to a bellowing roar.

"Go!" urged Jack.

Smoke billowed out of the cave. From its midst burst the dragon. His blue and green scales glittered, his spiky tail lashed side to side, his claws tore up the turf, and more smoke and fire jetted from his nostrils.

"Well done!" cried the boy.

The dragon winked.

streaming INTO
THE HILLS...

"Are you READY?"

FIRE jetted from
his NOSTRILS.

Saint George lowered his spear as his horse thundered over the turf. The dragon, enjoying the drama, reared and roared and rampaged back. There was a blur of golden armor and blue and green scales, and then the dragon's tail slammed the knight and horse back toward the cave.

Reared and ROARED and Rampaged BACk.

"He's making a good show of it," said Saint George to Jack, steadying his steed. The boy nodded and smiled, caught up in the excitement of it all.

Now the dragon was running around in circles, roaring and sending out gouts of flame and smoke. "Oo-oo-oo!" cried the onlookers, thrilled by the spectacle — as willing to cheer for the dragon as for their champion.

Saint George, with his spear lowered, charged again. But now the dragon leaped from side to side, with great thumps and bellows, confusing the warhorse, who suddenly turned aside. The saint barely held

saint George, with his spear lowered, charged again.

to the reins; the dragon bit off half of the steed's tail as he galloped by.

While the knight struggled to control his horse, the dragon strutted to and fro, puffing horsehair into the air like dandelion fluff. The crowd, always on the side of a winner, cheered again. The dragon basked in his new popularity.

Meanwhile, Jack made his way to where Saint George was adjusting his saddle and telling his horse exactly what he thought of his mount's sudden retreat. He dropped his voice to a mutter when he saw the boy approaching.

Adjusting his saddle...

What a splendid fight it's been," said Jack, "even if it's all play-acting."

"Play-acting," the man repeated thoughtfully, looking at his steed's shortened tail. "Yes, he's certainly putting a good front on things. Well, now might be the time to bring things

his steed's shortened tail.

"What a splendid fight it's been"

" THE FIGHT "
CONTINUES !

Trotted Toward
The Dragon...

... cracked his
Tail Like a whip.

to a close. Don't worry: I know the exact spot for the spear to go. After that, it's off to the feast for all of us."

Jack cupped his hands around his mouth and shouted, "The fight continues!"

To the dragon he gave a secret signal that meant "final round."

Saint George remounted his horse and trotted toward the dragon with his spear lowered. The dragon crouched and roared and cracked his tail like a whip. The knight began to circle, keeping his eye on the skin folds at the beast's throat.

The dragon, enjoying himself immensely, paced the horse and rider, sometimes darting his head at them and snapping his jaws so the horse canted back a pace or two. Jack and the crowd watched breathlessly.

The end came suddenly. Saint George charged. The dragon whirled around the knight in a confusion of spines, claws, tail, and churning dust. There was a roar. A flash of fire inside the dust cloud. Then silence. When the air cleared, the crowd applauded to see the dragon down, pinned to the earth by the spear point through a neck fold. The dismounted saint, atop the fallen creature, leaned one hand on the spear and raised his other arm in victory.

It seemed so real to Jack that the boy gave a cry and ran to the dragon's side. But he was reassured when the dragon lifted one large eyelid, winked, and then shut his eye again before anyone else noticed.

The End came suddenly

pinned to the Earth...

The Boy gave a cry and ran...

"AIN'T YOU GOIN' TO CUT HIS HEAD OFF?"

"Ain't you goin' to cut his head off?" asked the mayor, who came over to congratulate Saint George.

"Not today," said the knight pleasantly. "Let's all go down to the village and feast a bit. Then I'll give this creature a good talking-to, and you'll find that he'll be a very different dragon!"

At the word "feast," the crowd began streaming back toward town. Saint George released the dragon, who rose, shook himself, and

THE CROWD BEGAN STREAMING BACK TOWARD TOWN.

Jack lent him his handkerchief...

checked his spikes, claws and tail for damage. Jack lent him his
handkerchief so he could give his scales a quick dusting. "That was
a very good show!" said Jack.

"All in a day's work," the dragon replied. Then the saint climbed back
on his horse, and the dragon followed meekly with Jack beside him.

When the food and drink was gone, Saint George made a speech
in the village square.

The Dragon Followed meekly...

"I have removed the dreadful danger," he assured the townsfolk. "And the dragon has been thinking things over, and he isn't going to lay waste to the countryside any longer. He has also told me that if you are good to him, he might even settle down here — and that would be a very great distinction, indeed."

The crowd cheered as he sat down. The dragon, licking some meat pie off his claws, nudged Jack in the ribs and said, "Couldn't have put it better myself."

Everyone was happy. Saint George was pleased that he'd fought as he was obliged to, but that no one had been hurt (because he disliked killing, even though it was often his duty). The dragon was happy because he had enjoyed being the center of attention for much of the mock battle, and now he had become popular and could settle down peacefully. And Jack was happy because the pretend fight had been exciting. But, most importantly, he was happy that his two friends were unhurt and on the best of terms.

"I have Removed
The DREADFUL Danger"

The CROWD
cheered.

Licking some meat pie
OFF his claws...

The celebration continued into the evening. The dragon charmed them all with his learning and wit and good manners, and he proved the life of the party. When people began to drift home, Jack and the creature sat side by side on a doorstep, gazing at the sky. "Jolly stars! Jolly little town!" exclaimed the dragon. "I'm going to be ever so happy here."

With a contented sigh, Saint George sat down beside them. But Jack, worn out by the day's events, began nodding off, with his head resting against first the dragon, then the knight.

"Come along, my young friend," said the dragon. "Give me your hand. It's time you were home in bed. I'll walk you there."

"I'll stroll along, too," said Saint George, rising and taking Jack's other hand. So the three set off together: the saint, the dragon, and the boy. Though the lights in the village began to go out, there were the stars and a late moon to brighten their path. And as they turned the last corner and disappeared from view, they began to sing together, their three voices perfectly in tune.

THE DRAGON
charmed Them ALL...

gazing at the
sky.

Nodding
OFF...

T H E   E N D

HALTON HILLS PUBLIC LIBRARIES

3 1380 00259 1096